To Ciara –

Go have a great adventure!
😊

Susan Luban
2005

Noises AT Night

Noises AT Night

Beth Raisner Glass and Susan Lubner

illustrated by Bruce Whatley

HARRY N. ABRAMS, INC., PUBLISHERS

Designed by Elizabeth Morrow McKenzie
Production Manager: Jonathan Lopes

Library of Congress Cataloging-in-Publication Data

Glass, Beth Raisner.
Noises at night / by Beth Raisner Glass and Susan Lubner ; illustrated by Bruce Whatley.
p. cm.
Summary: A child imagines that the noises he hears at night, from a dripping faucet to the whistle of the wind, are really the
sounds of adventures in which he plays a sea captain, a policeman, and various other characters.
ISBN 0-8109-5750-7
[1. Noise—Fiction. 2. Night—Fiction. 3. Imagination—Fiction. 4. Adventure and adventurers—Fiction. 5. Stories in rhyme.]
I. Lubner, Susan. II. Whatley, Bruce, ill. III. Title.

PZ8.3.G42634No 2005
[E]—dc22
2004015455

Printed and bound in China
10 9 8 7 6 5 4 3 2 1

Harry N. Abrams, Inc.
100 Fifth Avenue
New York, NY 10011
www.abramsbooks.com

Abrams is a subsidiary of

LA MARTINIÈRE
GROUPE

For my sons, Will and Luke: Imagination is inspiration.
For my husband Mike: Your support means everything.
—BRG

~

To my little night owls, Hannah and Julia,
and to my husband, David, with love.
—SL

~

For Daniel, may your life be one big adventure.
—BW

When my room is dark and I snuggle in bed,
my eyes should be closed, but they're open instead.

I hear noises at night, they float through my house—
The bark of a dog and the scratch of a mouse.

I like to pretend when I shut off the light,
The noises turn into adventures at night!

DRRROPPP, DRRROPPP drips the faucet I hear down the hall,

It's not from the sink, but a ship sailing tall!

I stand at the helm—I'm a sea captain now,

I skim over waves that slap onto the bow.

Hisssss, Hisssss sighs the heater when it's getting hot,

The snake that I'll charm is curled up in a knot.

I play a sweet tune then the snake starts to dance,

He rises and sways himself into a trance.

VRROOOOMM, VRROOOOMM roars a truck as it drives through the rain,
And now I'm a pilot preparing my plane.
I rev up the engine—we're ready to fly,
We speed down the runway, then head for the sky.

Whieeee, Whieeee shrieks the wind as I pull up my sheet,

It's really the whistle I blow in the street!

For I'm a policeman in blue, head to toe,

Directing the traffic to stop and to go.

BOOOM, BOOOM rumbles thunder, my ears start to ring,

A drum roll is playing, I'm ready to swing!

I take a deep breath then I grab the trapeze,

I glide through the air as I hang from my knees.

Crreeak, Crreeak squeaks my bed when I turn on my side,

It's really a treasure chest opening wide.

I followed the map and I dug through the sand,

I am an explorer with gold in my hand!

TICCCKK, TOCCCKK goes the clock almost ready to chime,

I ride through the west, as my horse trots in time.

I round up the cattle and lasso a stray,

And hold down my hat as we gallop away.

Taaapp, Taaapp knocks a branch that falls down from a tree,

The crack of my bat makes the crowd cheer for me!

It's out of the park and I score the last run,

My teammates are shouting that I'm number one!

Shhh, Shhhhhh . . .

Can you hear it—the last noise at night?

It tiptoes around me and stays out of sight.

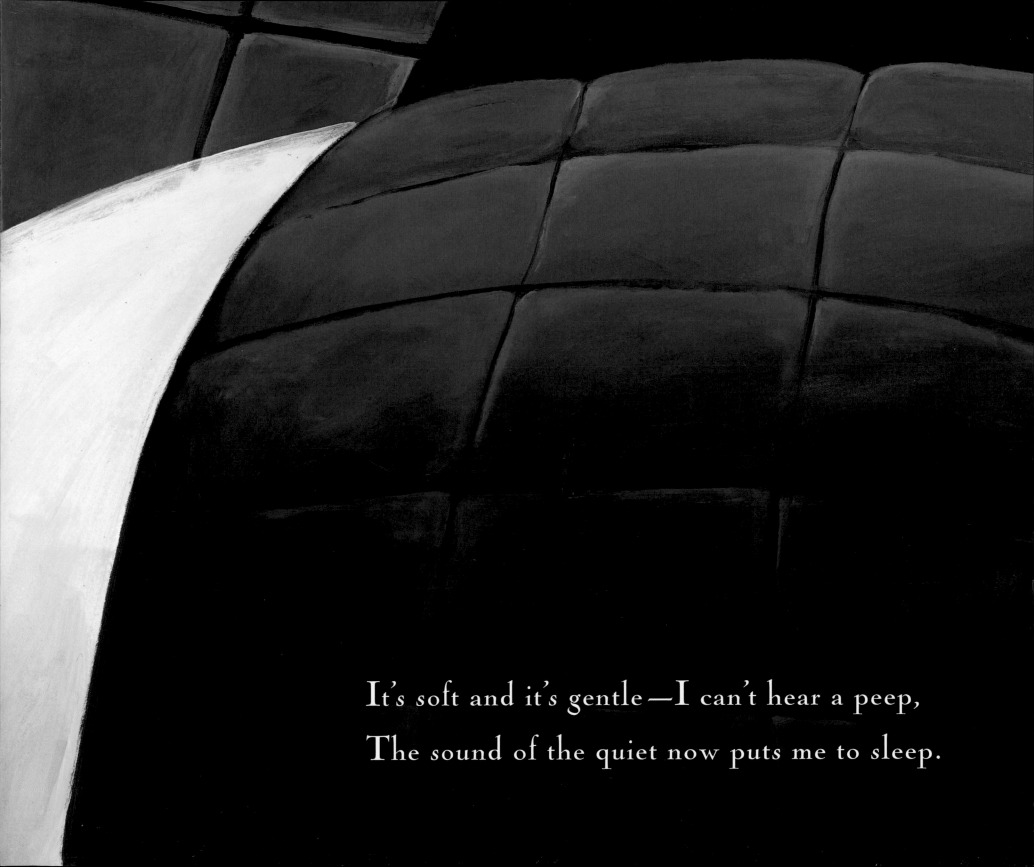

It's soft and it's gentle—I can't hear a peep,
The sound of the quiet now puts me to sleep.

Artist's Note

I like to work in a variety of mediums, choosing the one I feel suits the text best. For *Noises At Night,* I used acrylics, which allowed me to paint light on dark.

An illustrator has the special ability to add and extend the narrative through art. It's an opportunity to create different layers and moments of humor that appeal to kids one minute and parents the next. I am always looking for subplots that can support and complement the text—even creating characters who aren't mentioned in the text at all. (Sometimes I don't know how the authors put up with me!) But it's always a fun, collaborative process.

—Bruce Whatley

The authors would like to thank Tamar Brazis, Steven Cramer, Susan Goodman, Jackie Greene, and Maribeth Sanabria.